Happy sad

First published in Great Britain 1999
This edition published in 2002
by Egmont Books Limited
239 Kensington High St, London W8 6SA
Published in hardback by Heinemann Library,
a division of Reed Educational and Professional Publishing Ltd
by arrangement with Egmont Books Limited
Text copyright © Pippa Goodhart 1999
Illustrations copyright © Stephen Lambert 1999
The author and illustrator have asserted their moral rights
Paperback ISBN 1 4052 0487 7
Hardback ISBN 0 434 80278 6
10 9 8 7 6 5 4 3 2 1
A CIP catalogue record for this title
is available from the British Library.
Printed and bound in the U.A.E.

Pippa Goodhart

Happy Sad

Illustrated by Stephen Lambert

BLue Bananas

For

my friend Pauline

P.G.

To

Sarah, with love

S.L.

Toby lived by the sea. He loved it.
From his bedroom window he could
watch people on the sand and boats
on the water.

I can see
the sea.

On stormy days Toby walked in the wind
and watched the waves crashing
on the rocks.

On sunny days Toby took his sisters,

Daisy and Ellen, to the beach.

He chased them with wet seaweed.

When they were tired they made

sandcastles and ate sandy sandwiches.

7

But sometimes Toby liked to be alone with the sea. He liked to be there when the tide went out, leaving seaweed and surprises from its underwater world.

Wow!

Toby kept things he found from the sea.

He had a starfish

and a crab claw

and lots of shells.

Look what
I've found.

He even had a coconut.

One day Toby found a fishy tail flipping in a rock pool. He dipped in his net and fished out a mermaid.

Tears dripped down the mermaid's face.

'Why are you sad?' asked Toby.

'Because the tide pulled the sea away

and left me here!' cried the mermaid.

I want
to go home.

'Never mind,' said Toby.

'You come home

with me.'

So Toby gently lifted the mermaid and put her in his bag. Then he carried her home to show his family.

'What a pretty little thing,' said Mum,

giving the mermaid a cuddle.

'Let's get some water for her, to make her

feel at home,' said Dad.

So Dad filled the paddling

pool with water and

put the mermaid in.

She flipped her tail and swam

round the pool.

Look, a fountain.

Toby's sisters splashed and played with her.

Toby asked the mermaid, 'Are you happy now?'

'Oh, I am happy sad,' said the mermaid. 'I like the pool, but I miss my friends the fishes. In the sea, they used to swim and sing with me.'

'I'll get you a fish,' said Toby, and he took his money and went to the stalls on the seafront. He threw hoops and won a fish to be a friend for his mermaid.

Toby hurried home with

the little orange fish in a bag.

Toby tipped the fish

plop

into the pool.

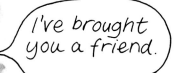

I've brought
you a friend.

Then he sat on the grass with his sisters
to watch. The little orange fish flipped its
tail and swam round the pool.

22

The mermaid sang a wavy wild song and splashed the fish. But the little fish just swam round and round. It didn't sing and it didn't play.

Oh, the song of the silvery sea. ♫♪♩♫

'Are you happy now?' asked Toby.

'I'm happy sad,' said the mermaid. 'I like the fish, but I miss, oh I miss, my father the sea. The salty, wavy sea that used to toss and play with me.'

'I'll make the pool like the sea,' said Toby, and he ran into the bathroom to get some seaweed shampoo.

He went to his bedroom to pick up some shells and stones.

Then he went down to the kitchen for a pot of salt.

What are you up to, Toby?

Toby ran back to the pool. He tipped in the shells and stones, the salt and seaweed shampoo. Then he put his hands into the water and stirred up waves and wildness.

'Are you happy now?' asked Toby.

'I'm still happy sad,' said the mermaid. 'I like the wildness, but I miss, oh I miss, my mother the sea. She used to rock me and sing me to sleep.'

'I can do that,' said Toby. He picked up
the mermaid. He held her in his arms.
He rocked her and he sang sleepy songs.

I miss my family.

But a tear ran down the mermaid's cheek.
'Oh, dear,' said Toby. 'Only the sea can
make you happy. I'll take you home.'

Toby's family waved goodbye as Toby
carried the little mermaid over
the sand to the sea.

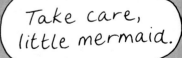

'Goodbye,' said Toby. 'I hope you will be happy now.'

The mermaid smiled. 'I am happy sad,' she said. 'I am happy because the salty wavy sea is my home. But I am sad to say goodbye to you. Why don't you come and live in the sea with me, Toby?

Then I won't be sad at all.'

Toby thought of having fishes for friends.

He thought of meeting Father sea and

Mother sea.

It would be fun living

with his mermaid friend.

But then Toby thought of his own father and mother.

He thought of leaving his little sisters.

He thought of his home
and his room, and he
shook his head.

'I want to go back to
my home too,' he said.

So the mermaid flipped her tail and

swam into the sea.

She dived down,

down,

down

and away.

Toby was sad as he watched her go,

but he was happy too. He was pleased

that the mermaid was happy.

Toby went back home. Daisy and Ellen were waiting for him. 'Let's play mermaid and fishes,' they said.

Then it was bedtime and Dad chased
them indoors. When Toby was tucked up
in bed, Mum sang him a mermaid song.

When Mum had said goodnight and gone downstairs, Toby listened to his big seashell and thought about the mermaid.

He looked out of his window at the
empty sand and sea. He looked along
the golden path of moonlight and saw
something. Was it the flick of a tail?
Could it be the wave of a hand?

Leabharlanna Dhún Laoghaire · Ráth An Dúin

I'm like the mermaid, thought Toby. I am happy sad. But the mermaid will always be my friend. Perhaps she will come back and play with me again.

And he snuggled down
in bed and went to sleep.